Harry's Home

Happy days, Lucian

Catherine and Laurence Anholt

ORCHARD BOOKS
96 Leonard Street, London EC2A 4XD
Orchard Books, Australia
14 Mars Road, Lane Cove, NSW 2066
Text © Laurence Anholt 1999
Illustrations © Catherine Anholt 1999
1 84121 033 1 (hardback)
1 84121 495 7 (paperback)
First published in Great Britain in 1999
The right of Laurence Anholt to be identified as the author
and Catherine Anholt to be identified as the illustrator
of this work has been asserted by them in accordance
with the Copyright, Designs and Patents Act 1988.
1 2 3 4 5 6 7 8 9 10 (hardback)
1 2 3 4 5 6 7 8 9 10 (paperback)
A CIP catalogue record of this book is
available from the British Library
Printed in Singapore

Harry's Home

Catherine and Laurence Anholt

ORCHARD BOOKS

Harry's home was in the city.

Harry loved the city. He loved escalators and lifts.
Shops and sirens. Big streets and little streets.
Traffic lights and fire-engines. He loved to see the
people rushing to work in the morning and coming
back to their homes in the evening.

Most of all, Harry loved to look at the city lights as he fell asleep at night.

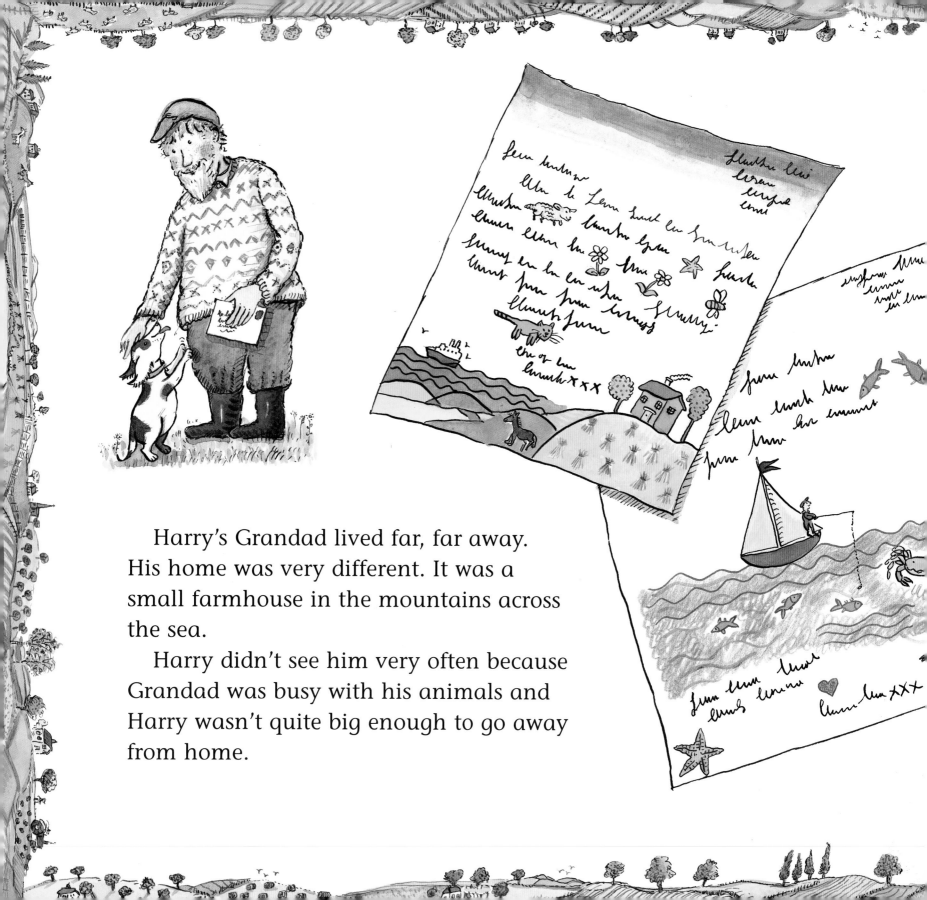

Harry's Grandad lived far, far away. His home was very different. It was a small farmhouse in the mountains across the sea.

Harry didn't see him very often because Grandad was busy with his animals and Harry wasn't quite big enough to go away from home.

Sometimes Grandad sent letters with little pictures for Harry. He told Harry about the mountains. He told Harry about the farm. He told Harry about looking after all the animals. Harry wished he could help too.

Then, on his birthday, Harry got a special parcel from Grandad.

Inside the parcel was a present.

Inside the present was a farm set.

Inside the farm set
was an envelope.

Inside the envelope
was a card.

Inside the card was...

...a train ticket!

At last! Harry was big enough.
Harry was going to Grandad's home.

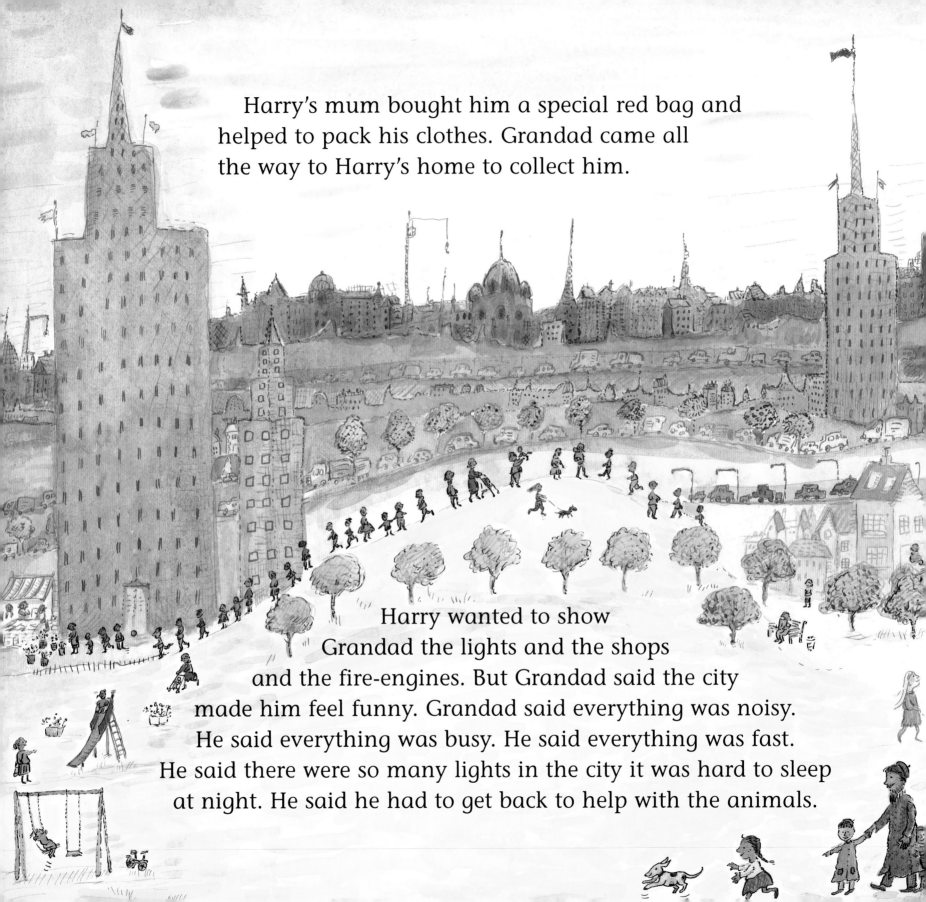

Harry's mum bought him a special red bag and helped to pack his clothes. Grandad came all the way to Harry's home to collect him.

Harry wanted to show Grandad the lights and the shops and the fire-engines. But Grandad said the city made him feel funny. Grandad said everything was noisy. He said everything was busy. He said everything was fast. He said there were so many lights in the city it was hard to sleep at night. He said he had to get back to help with the animals.

"It's time for me to go home," said Grandad.
"Come on Harry."
Then, for the very first time, Harry went away from
his mum. He took his special red bag and went away from
the city. For a whole week, Harry was going away from home.

They went on a bus.

They went on a train.

They went on a boat.

They went on another bus.

They went in a taxi.

And on the way Harry saw
LOTS of different kinds of homes,
where lots of different kinds of people lived.

"Here we are," said Grandad.

"There's no place like home."

Harry liked it at Grandad's home.

But it made him feel a little funny. Everything was quiet. Everything was slow. Everything was different. It was so dark that Harry couldn't sleep.

There was a wind blowing outside and Harry could hear sheep instead of cars and sirens.

Harry lay in his bed. He couldn't see any lights at all. He thought about his mum far, far away. He thought he would like to go home now. All the way back to his own home.

So Harry climbed out of bed and put all his clothes
back into the special red bag. Then he went downstairs
to tell Grandad.

"Oh Harry," smiled Grandad, lifting him onto his
lap. "You've only just arrived. We're going to have a
lovely week, just you wait and see."

Grandad told Harry he had
a surprise for him.

He took Harry by the hand
and led him into the kitchen.

In a warm spot in a corner of
the kitchen, was a wooden box.

Inside the wooden box
was a pile of straw.

And in the middle of
the straw, fast asleep,
was – a baby lamb.

Harry couldn't believe it. The lamb was as tiny as a toy.

"His mother couldn't feed him," said Grandad, picking up the lamb. "I thought you might like to look after him for the week."

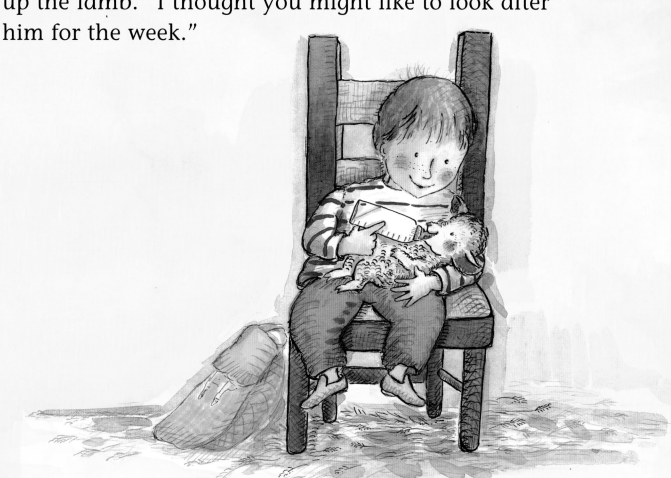

Harry put down his red bag and took the lamb. It was warm and soft as a pillow. Harry held it carefully. The little lamb put out a tiny pink tongue and sucked Harry's finger.

"It's hungry," said Grandad and gave Harry a baby's bottle with warm milk inside and showed Harry how to feed it.

Harry loved the lamb. The lamb loved Harry.
Every day at Grandad's home, Harry did
something new. Harry and his lamb saw lots of different
kinds of animals who lived in lots of different kinds of homes –

the pigs in the pigsty, the hens in the henhouse,

the doves in the dovecote, the cow in the barn,

the pony in the stable,   the dog in the kennel.

Harry liked looking after all the animals in their homes.
He liked it so much that he almost forgot about his own
home, far, far away in the city.

All week Harry helped in the farmyard.

"The week has gone so fast," said Grandad, as they packed Harry's special red bag. "Tomorrow you'll be going home. All the way back to the city, and I will miss you."

Harry would miss his Grandad too. He wondered how he would carry his lamb on the bus and on the train. Perhaps Grandad could give him a dog-lead.

"Oh no," smiled Grandad. "Lambs belong here in the country, like me. You see, Harry, everyone has their own home."

Harry followed Grandad. They walked down the lane
into the fields with the lamb dancing along behind.
Harry thought about his lamb in the city.

Grandad was right. The lamb wouldn't like fire-engines.
It wouldn't like escalators.

Suddenly a big sheep came right over to Harry. "Look,
Harry," said Grandad, "I think this is the mother sheep."

Harry thought for a moment and looked at his little
lamb. Then he gently put it down onto the grass.
With a flip of its tail, the lamb was gone.

Harry had been big enough to go away from home.
He loved it with Grandad, but now he wanted to go
home too. Just like the lamb.
Someone was waiting at the farmhouse . . .

Harry ran indoors and gave his mum such a big hug that she almost fell over.

Then Grandad told Harry's mum how Harry had looked after the lamb all on his own and let it go back into the field. His mum gave him a squeeze and said she was very proud of him.

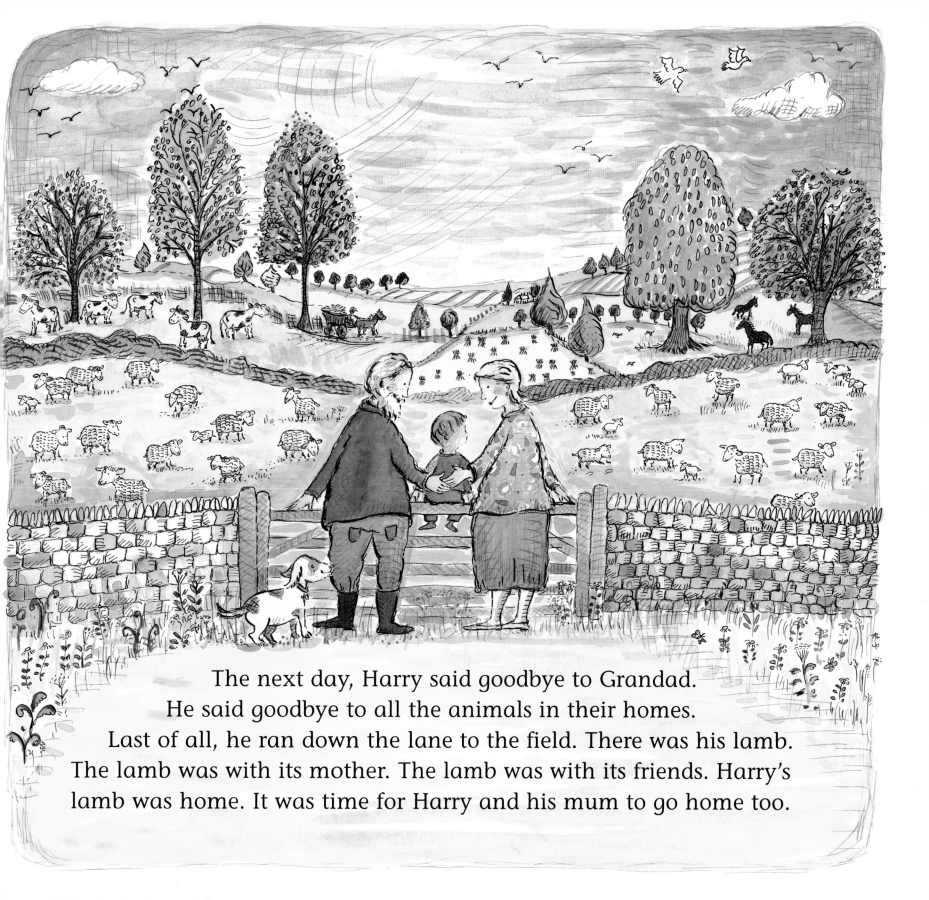

The next day, Harry said goodbye to Grandad.
He said goodbye to all the animals in their homes.
Last of all, he ran down the lane to the field. There was his lamb.
The lamb was with its mother. The lamb was with its friends. Harry's
lamb was home. It was time for Harry and his mum to go home too.

They went in a taxi.

They went on a bus.

They went on a boat.

They went on a train.

They went on another bus.

And on the way Harry saw
LOTS of different kinds of homes,
where lots of different kinds of people lived.

But there was only one home that was quite right for Harry –

And that was . . .

Harry's home.